I'LL NEVER TELL

AND OTHER SHORT STORIES

ALSO BY RICK TREON

<u>Bartholomew Beck Thrillers</u>

LIVE WITH THE TRUTH

LET THE GUILTY PAY

THE PRICE OF SILENCE

<u>Political Thrillers</u>

DEEP BACKGROUND

DIVIDED STATES

PRAISE FOR RICK TREON

"Rick Treon dispenses well-earned twists and reveals with the stiletto precision of a master."
—*USA Today* bestselling author
Heather Young

"Rick Treon does a wonderful job with misdirection and suspense."
—PEN Southwest Book Award winner
Chera Hammons

"I read (*Let the Guilty Pay*) in one day, something I almost never do. It was expertly paced, the characters distinct, and the twists surprising."
—Heather Chavez, author of
Blood Will Tell

"Treon knows how to crank up the tension..."
—*Lone Star Literary*

I'LL NEVER TELL

AND OTHER SHORT STORIES

RICK TREON

BOMB CITY ENTERTAINMENT

I'LL NEVER TELL: AND OTHER SHORT STORIES

by Rick Treon

Published by Bomb City Entertainment, LLC

ISBN: 979-8-99-009211-2

TABLE OF CONTENTS

I'LL NEVER TELL

BROTHER

They'll never find Finn Bowman's body. I should know; I buried him. Sure, I had some help. But if it ever comes up, she was never here.

To answer your question: No, Finn's death wasn't my fault.

But we have plenty of time to discuss that. First, I need to get the hell out of here. Not because I need to outrun anyone. I was too careful for that. But I have a passenger in the truck, and she needs to get to school. My sister's absence would cause worry and put the whole town on edge by lunch.

Finn missing work won't trip any wires for at least two days.

My diesel's turbo whines like a jet engine about to take off. And if she's going to make it to the front door, I'll damn near have to make this dually fly.

"Did we really have to go so far?" she asks. "I mean, we left them a trail in the other direction, pushed his truck into a playa lake in yet another direction, then buried him more than a mile from any of the lease roads. You don't think that's a bit much?"

I shake my head.

"Whatever. There's no way anyone would've found him even fifty yards off any trail."

"I don't think some roughneck or rancher will stumble on his body. But the bugs'll come, even though we buried him. It's too shallow. And those bugs'll attract bigger critters, and that'll bring the coyotes. But it's mostly okay until the vultures come around, waiting to pick the bones clean. Because once people know Finn's gone missing, circling vultures'll be a red flag for the roughnecks and the ranchers, and they'll call the sheriff. But if the grave is remote enough, the vultures might be too far away for anyone from the road to see."

She sighs and curls up in the seat, her head resting on the glass of the passenger window. She's a senior and captain of the track team—her cardio came in handy because burying that big sonofabitch took forever, even in a shallow grave—so I sometimes forget my little sister can still be vulnerable.

I SLAM ON my brakes with less than two minutes before the first bell. She'd woken up an hour ago and hopped in the back to change. Though she won't be her freshest, waking up late and skipping a shower is plausible.

As for why I'm driving her to school when she has a restored Ford Bronco that's the envy of half the school? Well, it's vintage, and I was over trying to fix it before we finally gave up. That may also help explain why she'll be anxious and agitated all day.

"Try and pretend it was a bad dream," I say.

She doesn't respond, just slams the truck door and runs toward the entrance. I hear the bell ring before I turn the corner toward town.

Toward Finn's house.

While my truck's presence in front of the school was odd—I graduated two years ago and haven't driven by campus since—parking on the curb next to Finn's front yard will be expected. So will be unlocking his front door and walking inside.

Finn and I are brothers. I was always the more

responsible one, so every morning I drive by and wake him up for work, even though it means I have to speed to get to my jobsite on time. I've been doing it for almost a year now. The trade-off is getting his full rent check every month. I barely make anything off the property, what with the friends and family rate I charge. But divorce sucks, and I was more than happy to break even on the deal if it would get him to finally leave her.

But divorce also makes a man feel free to act on his impulses, the ones he's been suppressing. And he was good at hiding them.

And we're brothers.

Were brothers.

Guess I'll have to get used to that.

Whoever Finn really was, I'm in his house because I know my sister left something in his house during the night in question. Her driver's license, of all things.

Thank God she got out of there before things really got out of control.

SISTER

I couldn't tell him the truth. I wouldn't have been able to control the situation, and he'd be in jail right now instead of finding my stupid freaking ID while I'm stuck studying stupid freaking Shakespeare in this stupid freaking classroom.

I can't tell you the truth, either. I mean, why would I? We don't even know each other.

But here's the official story, the one I'm telling till I'm dead as that SOB we just buried.

My bro never drank much, and now that he's supporting us both he really doesn't risk being too hung over for work. So, he left the party at about ten, though it hadn't turned into much of anything so early on a Thursday night—which is when the college kids start their weekends.

No, I'm not a college kid. And neither is my

bro or Finn, the dirt bag I grew up calling brother. Not that I could see he was a dirtbag until it happened. But sometimes it's like that— you don't see the most obvious things until someone points them out.

Anyways, my real brother and I went over because it was the one-month anniversary of Finn's divorce being finalized. Finn was staying in one of my bro's rent houses because she got their McMansion and land on the edge of town. And though my bro and I'd never say it, she deserved it. She made most of the money to buy it. Finn had been treating the rent house like Party Central since moving in. I'd been to one of the gatherings—don't you dare tell my bro—and everything had been pretty chill. Mostly guys from Finn's graduating class, but a few girls from the local community college who weren't quite twenty-one yet. Nobody still in high school.

But apparently the invite list was expanded for his divorcé soiree. Or word had just gotten around about Party Central.

Either way, Bianca Gomez and a few of her Mean Girls were there. Though they intimidated a lot of the girls, I got along with them just fine. We were all-state athletes—they play softball— and respected each other. But that's where the similarities end. Bianca and her drones are more

... experienced than me, which is how I like it. But I don't judge them. And neither should you, got it? And in any case, at about two in the morning (Queen) B said of all the dudes at that party, there wasn't one she would screw—my word; she used the one you were probably thinking.

Her two friends and I were the only ones who heard that. Finn and his guys were all out back getting baked, and we were the only girls left. I don't smoke anything, and the rest weren't out there because the school tests all athletes.

When Finn and his guys came back in, they were too much. Too drunk. Too high. Too obnoxious. With his buddies laughing in the background, he asked us all to pull out our IDs. They wanted to see who was of age.

I knew it was dumb to play along, but I figured if I just did what they asked, they'd move on. But after one of the other guys took it from me and winked—I just turned eighteen—I peaced out and walked home. Didn't even bother to take the ID back. I invited B and her drones to come over for some frozen pizza, but B said they were gonna hang a while longer.

The next day, B came to me and said Finn's friends decided they couldn't go through with it. They'd apparently thought they could turn it into a sex party since there were three of them and three girls left. But when B called their bluff, they acted like most guys and left.

Except for Finn.

B went into details that no other person alive will ever hear. She swore she'd never tell anyone else what happened, but she begged me to make Finn pay. So I begged my brother. But he started the evening as the levelheaded grown man he'd been since about seven years old.

So I forced his hand. I snuck over to Finn's place and asked him to take me somewhere secluded so we could drink and have a good time.

Then I texted my brother a photo of Finn slumped against his steering wheel, blood and brain splattered on his driver's side window.

Next came the caption. Need help.

Then I dropped him a location pin.

BROTHER

I found her license in the corner of Finn's bedroom, like it had been flung there.

Weird.

That got me curious, so I started looking around the room for anything else that seemed weird. The search ended with me taking a look under Finn's bed.

And now I'm holding one of her sports bras. I know it's hers because I ordered them online—it's the same brand, size, and crazy pink-purple-green camo pattern. It also has her initials written in sharpie on the back because thievery is apparently a problem in the girls' locker room.

She offered to get a job after our piece of shit father abandoned us after Mom died, but I told her my construction job and side hustles could get us through. She'd have to get that track scholarship if she wanted a college education, but that had been a foregone conclusion since she started sprinting and long jumping in eighth grade.

The underwear was a gift for her birthday.

Now it's proof that things did not go down like she said.

WHEN SHE WALKS in after practice, I'm sitting in my leather loveseat. I replaced our old man's ratty microfiber chair two weeks after reading his note.

Your grown enuff.

He dropped out after eighth grade to go work the oilfields with his foreman father, and Permian Basin cops didn't bother with truancy back then. My sister found the note and texted me a photo, then a message.

Good riddance. And now you can move back and stop paying rent!

She didn't know the old man was two months behind on the mortgage, which still had five years left.

Six months later, I'm sitting in my still-new-feeling recliner, a cold beer in my right hand, the third of eighteen 'Stones she and I are likely to kill tonight. I normally keep it to six and make sure she stays sober since it's track season.

Tonight will be an exception.

In my left hand, I hold her bra—initials out, so she knows I know.

But she still tries to play it off. "Bro, why are you holding my underwear? That's weird."

"Stop."

"I know you have to dig into my stuff to keep me honest, but seriously."

"You didn't have to lie to me like that."

"Bro—"

"Goddammit, if you don't cut it out, I swear I'll—"

She takes a defiant step toward me. "What? Hit me? Like he did? In the stomach so I'll puke but nobody will see the bruises?"

Heat rushes to my face. The old man never did it while I was around or I'd've put a stop to it real fucking quick. But after I graduated and Mom started fading, he had free reign. When I moved back in, she told me about the abuse. I almost went on a revenge quest but thought better of it. We were better off with him gone. And if he ever comes back, there's that unregistered eight-shot revolver he thought he'd hidden in his closet. I put it back, thinking it was my secret.

But my sister had known it was there for years. She'd also made sure it still worked before taking it out there last night to exact the revenge I wouldn't. Like I told her when she first came to be with the story about what Finn had done, I didn't believe it was my place to kill anyone. Bianca isn't my sister.

But now?

Now, I have no idea what I believe.

SISTER

You'll never know what happened that night. And neither will my bro. But the bad guy's dead, and I'm holding an envelope my track coach gave me after practice. Inside, there's a scholarship offer from South Plains College. Everything's going to plan.

All I have to do now is keep surviving.

THE OTHER MAN'S DAUGHTER

My head ached. No, that doesn't quite describe it. If it were a run-of-the-mill needle behind the eye, it wouldn't be worth talking about. But my brain was swelling, expanding beyond the limits of my skull.

Tears made it difficult to navigate, so I pulled over at a gas station and walked to the front passenger side. My shoulders slumped when I saw the donut. It wasn't a dream. Part of me thought the twenty minutes I spent changing the flat was a hallucination.

My phone buzzed as I paid for three packages of Tylenol. The number wasn't in my contacts, but the words were intimate.

Don't go home. She's getting worse so we

went back to the hospital. Hurry.

I formulated a reply while popping all six pills and washing them down with an energy drink.

I think you have the wrong number. Hope everything works out OK.

I'd just put my pickup in reverse when I got a response.

R U kidding? Our daughter is dying Odie. Quit being a shitbag. Meet us at the hospital.

I stared at the text until honking brought me back. This person knew my nickname, the one reserved for my closest friends. And she—I assumed it was a woman on the other end—said we had a daughter together. A gravely ill daughter.

I had nowhere pressing to go. Netflix, leftovers, and a bottle of Jameson were all that waited in my one-bedroom apartment. And even if one of my friends was playing a morbid trick on me, maybe a doctor could tell me what the hell was wrong with my head. That alone was worth a one-letter text.

K

LACKING A NAME to ask for, I told the nurse I was there to see the woman with a sick baby. He tilted his head and rested a reassuring hand on my arm. He led me through a maze of halls until stopping before a room with Delilah written on the whiteboard. The name meant nothing to me, but I stepped inside, hoping to put the issue to rest.

Then I saw Delilah's mother.

An instant became three years, and I had the memories of two men. Both of us had met the woman at a bar on Main Street. She was staying overnight on her way to Boulder for her senior year. Both men went back to her hotel and fell in love.

The next morning was the moment of mitosis, when my brain cells divided and the other man was born. I said goodbye and didn't bother to get the woman's number. The other man begged her to stay. Just one semester off, enough time for him to find work in Colorado.

The other man made love with the woman every night for a year in their new home. She released in him the creativity he'd tried for years to find. He finished the screenplay he always talked about writing, and it took just a few months to sell. But on the day he got the news, the woman wanted to celebrate something else. Delilah.

With the prospect of a new life in Hollywood, the other man left. He paid her bills and stopped in for major events and holidays when his schedule allowed. He partied and hobnobbed and was the ultimate Good Time Charlie. He went to rehab. Twice.

He also had a dying daughter he didn't want to deal with.

I, on the other hand, had left the hotel room with a constant weight of regret. Was she the one? I tried later to look her up but got nowhere. Between then and now, I'd gotten two promotions and four raises at work. I should've had a nice house with a two-car garage and enough vehicles to fill it, plus an RV parked out front. My laptop had a file on it named Million Dollar Screenplay, but I hadn't opened it in months. At night I drove home wanting more out of life but lacking the motivation to do anything.

I didn't want to die but I hated living. I dreamed every evening about a wrong-way trucker taking me out on the Canadian River bridge, wishing someone else would do what I lacked the courage to.

"IT'S ABOUT TIME," the woman said. "Your plane landed four hours ago."

Of all the memories I now possessed, that one was missing. The other man's past stopped the night before. He was released from the inpatient facility and drove to the nearest liquor store, got blackout drunk, and was never heard from again.

But the woman was expecting an explanation, and I had one. "I had a flat. It took forever to get back on the road."

She stepped forward to smell me. She seemed surprised by the lack of liquor on my breath, and for a moment I felt the spark we shared. I reached for her but was interrupted by a doctor.

"Is this the father?" the doctor asked. The two women knew each other and had already formed an opinion about the other man. And they were right.

Delilah's mother and the doctor turned their backs and began discussing the baby's ailment. There was no room in the conversation for an absentee father, so I walked over to the other man's daughter.

But the baby's nose and eyes were mine, and I knew she wasn't just his daughter. She was my daughter, too. My head began ringing, so I shut my eyes and screamed before being shoved aside by the doctor and two nurses.

The ringing wasn't in my head. It was Delilah's heart monitor flatlining.

I HELD MY face and sobbed alone in the waiting room. Was I me, or was I the other man? Hadn't I worked my shift that day? Hadn't I changed that flat tire? Or was I the man who'd abandoned his dying daughter?

His dead daughter.

Still unsure of my reality, I pried my face from tear-soaked hands. But they weren't wet from crying. They were slick with blood. I spun around in a blind panic, calling for a doctor. I stood and staggered toward the nurse's station, yelling but getting nothing in response.

I was about to grab one by the arm when a white-hot hand gripped my shoulder. I fell to the tiled floor in pain and looked behind me at the man in the scarlet suit. Like I had with Delilah's mother, I knew him instantly. My head was freed of pain while the hospital fluttered away like ash, replaced by a black expanse of pain and regret.

"Did you get what you wanted?" the man in the scarlet suit asked.

His question was rhetorical. I hadn't asked him for anything. Not explicitly. But while wishing for an act of God to take me out on the drive home, he had shown up. Instead of letting the wrong-way driver kill me, I swerved, my front tire nicking the concrete barrier just right.

The man in the scarlet suit knelt beside me as I pumped the jack. I confessed to him my darkest thoughts and deepest desires. I described the life I wanted. I told him about the woman.

He offered me three choices. He could take me to my past, to that morning in the hotel room, and let me carve out the life I'd coveted to the point of depression. He could show me what that past had been and where I would be now, but I would return to the life I despised. Or he could kill me.

I WOKE UP lying on the road, a man shaking me. The trucker. The real trucker, not the man in the scarlet suit.

"Are you okay? I can drive you to the hospital."

I looked down at my hands. No blood. My shoulder burned, but I knew what that was from. I smiled and declined the invitation.

I wasn't the other man. I was me, but finally free of my pasts. The one I'd lived—and the one I hadn't.

HIS AND HERS

I t was five till five and I was feeling whistle-bit when a tall septuagenarian in a three-piece suit walked in. I hoped he was there for Gloria, the founding partner of Ramirez & Associates.

She didn't have any associates.

I wasn't technically on Gloria's payroll, but I did investigative work in exchange for my windowless cubby and waferboard desk. We were college buddies—I flirted with becoming an attorney before I discovered the occupation had nothing to do with the law—who preferred a similar clientele.

But after checking a gold pocket watch and replacing it in his vest pocket, all the old man said was, "Howdy, ma'am. I'm looking for Mr. Cooper McSwain."

My door was open.

Rookie mistake.

There was no use hiding, so I squeezed around my desk and walked out, ready to shoot him down quick. "Folks call me Coop. What can I do for you?"

The old man looked me up and down. "Nice jeans."

I nodded in thanks. There aren't many private investigators in Amarillo, and I'm the only one who wears jeans with heavy starch and a crease. That shouldn't be noteworthy in a city where statues of painted horses are considered municipal beautification, but my pants are usually the first thing people comment on when we meet.

I don't wear them to make a fashion statement, though I suppose they are symbolic in a way. I wear them because I'm one of the few private eyes in town willing to take cases out on the ranches and oil leases in the Panhandle. I'd rather catch a cattle rustler—yes, those still exist—or a pumpjack saboteur than get photos of some CEO's cheating spouse. Those who wear white collars have never interested me.

Not my people. Not my problem.

That's what made this encounter even more irritating than a normal Friday evening walk-in.

"I have a domestic situation I'd like investigated."

Of course he did. "I see. Well, mister ... I apologize, but I didn't catch your name."

"Whitehead. George T. Whitehead. I work in the—"

"Chase Tower."

"FirstBank Southwest Tower."

I improved my posture out of reflex while he corrected me. "Right. Old habit."

A corner of his mouth ticked up. "You're too young to have old habits."

I mirrored his expression, thankful I hadn't gotten on his bad side. Whitehead was the oldest grandson in one of Amarillo's founding families, the heir to an oil fortune that put him on the same Forbes list as Robert F. Smith and Jacqueline Mars. He didn't work in Amarillo's tallest building. He owned two floors.

The money didn't impress me. It's the damage he could do with it that made me edgy.

Whitehead was also married to one of the city's most beloved women, Wendy Whitehead. Her philanthropic efforts have helped countless families in these parts. And she was older than George, so I had a hard time picturing her involved in anything torrid enough to require my services.

"You said you had a domestic situation?"

"Yes." Whitehead looked at Gloria, who was

packing her briefcase as slowly as possible. "Can we take this into your office, Mr. McSwain?"

The thought of going back into the cramped room made me wince. "Can we take a walk instead?"

We agreed to a stroll back to the tower. I could get a pick-me-up at the coffee shop in the lobby, so my time wouldn't be completely wasted.

Ramirez & Associates is a few blocks west and south of the only building in the city that could be confused with a skyscraper, but it's ten floors and more than a hundred feet short of hitting the mark. Gloria's single-story stucco building was about that far away from housing an elite law firm.

But her location was strategic. It was only a few blocks away from the Downtown Women's Center, two pawn shops, and three bail bondsmen. We both preferred helping those in more desperate need of sound legal and investigative assistance. And when we did take cases for the money, we made sure the clients were honest folk, which usually meant they lived outside the city limits.

Gorge T. Whitehead fit neither of those descriptions.

It took ten steps for me to get to the point. "What can I help you with that the police or a lawyer can't?"

We passed a vagrant underneath the ruins of an ancient service station. This side of downtown had yet to experience the effects of Amarillo's decades-long revitalization efforts, and most of the buildings were abandoned and needed razing. I eyed Whitehead, expecting him to look at the man with fear or disgust. But to my surprise, the oil baron nodded at the homeless man and his grocery cart, then carried on with our conversation.

"The police have helped me with their end. What I seek now is resolution of a more personal nature."

And there it was. The old man probably had baggies full of blue pills stashed on his floors and wanted to use them without giving his wife fifty percent. As though he couldn't live for another ten years on half a billion.

"Just so we're clear, I don't help people obstruct justice. If that's what you're after, I can refer you to someone who might be willing—"

"You're misunderstanding me, Mr. McSwain." Whitehead stopped and turned to me. "I'll start from the beginning."

By the time we reached his black Range Rover, my take on George T. Whitehead had changed. In addition to his oil fortune, the old man had owned a sprawling ranch northeast of the city, near Pampa. He went there every weekend and for a month every summer. His daughter, Grace, spent even more time there. It had always been more her home than Whitehead Hall out in Tascosa Hills.

That's why he transferred ownership when Grace turned twenty-five. By then she'd already earned a bachelor's in animal husbandry and a master's in animal science from Texas A&M. The place was now one of the finest equestrian refuges in the state that doubled as a dude ranch from June through August.

George and Wendy didn't have much to do with the ranch anymore, save for occasional visits and storage. But items stored by billionaires tend to be more valuable than what the rest of us hide.

George Whitehead kept a safe in the ranch's bunkhouse. It was hidden underneath the floorboards, and only George and Wendy knew it was there or had the combination. Inside was cash, bonds, gold bars, and the family jewels. Of particular value were two diamond necklaces, a matching pair that were essentially priceless.

And all of it was gone.

Grace had called George a week ago in a panic after her foreman, a cowboy named Jake, found his floorboards pried open, revealing the empty safe. George called the police and his high-dollar lawyer, and they took note of everything that was stolen. The ranch's insurance was now Grace's, so she was due millions. The only items the insurers had refused to cover were the necklaces.

"And that was fine by me," George said. "They were mostly sentimental. And it's not like they could be replaced, even if we were given the money to do so."

"I'm sorry to hear about all of that." I surprised myself by telling the truth. I'd dealt with many rich jackholes trying to get over on working-class folk, leaving me with a strong bias against men like George Whitehead. But it turns out he was a family man who tried to do right by his wife and daughter.

Still, one question remained.

"What does any of this have to do with me?"

"The sheriff arrested Jake, but he's wrong." He furrowed his brow. "The ranch is secluded, and it hasn't been open for guests in more than a month, so they figured he must've done it. Grace put up the bond, of course, so he's already out. The thing is, I don't know where Jake could go with the gold and bonds without them being traced back to him. I suppose he could spend the cash, but he doesn't know anything about laundering money."

I was beginning to understand George's trusting nature. But who else could've done it, other than his daughter?

"So who do you think could've done it?"

George closed his eyes for a long moment. When he opened them, they were red. "I think it might've been Grace."

Trusting, but not blind.

"And she made it look like a robbery to get the insurance money."

He nodded.

"I take it the ranch is in financial trouble."

"It's always been a money pit. She knew I'd give her all the money in the world to keep it running, but I don't think she appreciated having to rely on me. And I won't mind if she committed the insurance fraud. I just want the necklaces. They've been in my family for generations, Mr. McSwain." He opened the door to his Range Rover. "If you can convince her to make them reappear, I'll make it well worth your time."

This was the definition of a family matter, and I had every reason to stay out of it.

"Why are you coming to me with this?"

"You probably know this already, but you've got quite a reputation in my circle. You go out of your way to stick it to us capitalists, and you prefer people who live and work out in the country. In this case, I hope keeping that ranch afloat and bilking the insurance company will appeal to your nature."

"And what about Jake?"

"I can keep him out of jail."

Gorge was right about that. The criminal justice system allows for more crime and provides little justice when it comes to the super-rich.

"Okay, Mr. Whitehead, I'll see what I can do. My standard fee—"

"Just send me an invoice when you're done. Expense everything, and don't be afraid to overbill me."

He gave me the directions to his ranch, and we shook hands. I could use the money. And so long as he kept Jake out of jail, I had no problem finding his necklaces and letting the giant insurance firm give his daughter a few million to keep her noble enterprise afloat.

I FELT MORE at home on Ranch-to-Market Road 2391 than I ever did in the city. I lived in an apartment on Polk Street, a shoebox on the third floor of a renovated historic building reserved for Section 8 housing. I qualified by not reporting any of my cash clients and writing everything off as a business expense, including the nonexistent office rent. The claustrophobia of the city is probably why I loved driving my old cherry red Ford pickup, climbing the green hills between Pampa and Miami after record rainfall in the spring and summer.

As I crested the last hill before the turnoff for Grace's ranch, I passed a black Range Rover, an exact duplicate of the one I'd seen just over an hour ago. It couldn't be George. It was going too fast to make out the driver, but I suspected it was Wendy.

The ranch was about a mile off RM 2391, though you could see it a few hundred yards after crossing the cattle guard. I was within a football field when I saw a young woman in a straw hat and denim collared shirt run out of the main house toward what I assumed was the bunkhouse in question. The woman—Grace, I assumed—was at a dead sprint, so I sped up to meet her at the smaller building, which was still about the size of the law offices of Ramirez & Associates.

I burst in a few seconds after Grace and found her weeping over the shirtless body of a young man in a leather recliner.

I CALLED THE Gray County sheriff, then tried to

calm Grace. She sat on a couch opposite the boy, who she identified as Jake. I didn't have any latex gloves on me or in the pickup, so I couldn't do much poking around before the sheriff arrived.

But a superficial investigation pointed to suicide. His right hand was still clutching a black semi-automatic pistol, and it appeared a bullet had entered his right temple and exited the left. On the nightstand were two sheets of paper underneath a half-empty whiskey bottle.

I sat down next to Grace, who had replaced tears with a thousand-yard stare. "So, you heard the shot and came running out, right as I was pulling up?"

She nodded but didn't say anything.

"And your mother, she was here with you a few minutes earlier, right?"

Another nod. More silence.

"Was Jake with you two?"

Grace shook her head. "We thought he was working the ranch. His truck isn't parked outside, but he must've driven one of the UTVs out there."

I've never been good at comforting people, but I put my hand on Grace's back. I was about to ask if she'd seen this coming when the sheriff walked in.

I stayed as he and a deputy processed the

scene and called for a forensics team. The sheriff and I read the suicide note together, wherein Jake apologized for stealing the items but said the guilt of lying to everyone was too much. The second sheet of paper was a treasure map showing where he'd buried the items from the safe.

The sun had set by the time we found his X. The Gray County boys set up lights and started digging. The goods weren't very deep. Jake had stashed it in two blue duffel bags—one with gold, the other stuffed with cash and bonds.

Neither had the diamond necklaces.

The deputies dug for another hour, then sifted through the dirt piles by hand, but the diamonds were not among the rest of Jake's loot.

When we got back to the bunkhouse, another piece of evidence had been located. The crime scene techs had found another hand-drawn map in Jake's desk. This one showed the building's floor plan and indicated the square where Jake could pry up the floorboards and find the safe. Below that were three numbers, which we agreed was the combination to the safe. The most telling information, though, was at the top of the page.

The map had been drawn on a piece of fancy letterhead belonging to one George T. Whitehead.

THE AMARILLO POLICE Department made a big show of arresting George. They surrounded the Chase Tower parking lot on Saturday morning as though they expected him to come out shooting. The Potter County DA was in attendance for the perp walk, as were all three news stations and a lonely newspaper reporter. She only knew because the police had told everyone to evacuate the tower, including the four-person newsroom.

Gloria was tipped off by a friendly cop, so we also stopped by. George was led out in handcuffs. He looked calm, scanning the crowd until we made eye contact. Despite seeing the evidence myself, I couldn't find the deceit in his eyes.

What APD found in his offices, however, finally convinced me of his guilt. I'd been right about the little blue pills. He had bottles of them, along with prescription narcotics and photos of various women he'd slept with on his floors of the tower. George may have been a good father, but he was a cowpie of a husband and obviously not as righteous as I thought.

"IS THAT WHAT you're wearing, Coop?" Gloria looked me up and down, but we both knew what she was referring to.

"I haven't worn anything but starched blue

jeans since the day I moved back. What makes you think I'll change now?"

"Well, it is a funeral."

I shook my head. "I'm wearing a button-down collar with a Men's Warehouse tie and my good Stetson. That's dressy enough."

She was about to keep arguing when her phone buzzed. "The grand jury indicted Whitehead on illegal possession of prescription drugs and conspiracy to commit insurance fraud."

"That was fast." It was only Monday, but the DA had been hot to get one of Amarillo's elites on the docket.

Whitehead must've donated to the other guy last election.

Despite the fact he'd stolen her family's treasure and killed himself, Wendy Whitehead insisted Jake receive a proper funeral service at First Baptist. It was only a few cobblestone blocks south of Gloria's offices, so we walked and became two of about a thousand still streaming into the church.

We huddled near the back with the standing-room-only crowd and listened as the preacher spoke, followed by various members of Jake's family.

Then it was Grace's turn. She was dressed in

black and looked every bit the part of a grieving widow, which she wasn't.

"First, I'd like to thank everyone for coming. I know many of you didn't know Jake personally, but I appreciate you supporting my family and me. These last few days have been tough. And even though it wasn't something we publicized, Jake and I were in love."

I'd suspected as much, but an audible whisper spread among pews.

"In fact, I thought Jake was going to propose to me. I'd been waiting forever for it." She smiled and wiped away a tear. "I even heard he went to a jewelry store all the way in Oklahoma City. I assume he was going to buy me a ring there, but he never got the chance."

Why Oklahoma City? There were plenty of good places to get engagement rings in Amarillo. What's the advantage?

"Jake was also close with my father. Any time he could get off the ranch, he'd spend it with Dad in his offices or out at the house with him and my mother."

The answer to my question started coming into focus.

Casinos.

It's one of the best places to launder money, so long as you have the patience to do it in small enough increments to avoid taxes and alerting the IRS. And if you can prove you like a casino before a robbery has been committed, that's even more proof you weren't there to clean stolen bills. Jake probably had a lead on a shady diamond dealer there, too.

Grace stepped away, and the preacher closed the service with more scripture. Gloria left for her office, but I thought giving my condolences to Grace was the right thing to do. After waiting for nearly twenty minutes outside the church, I finally stepped up to her and Wendy.

"It was a beautiful service." I took Grace's hand and wrapped it with both of mine. "And again, I'm so sorry for your loss."

"Thank you." The smile on her face made me feel a bit less awkward. "And thank you so much for assisting the sheriff's office out there."

"Well, I don't know if it made much of a difference." I looked at Wendy. "I'm just glad Jake waited for you to leave, Mrs. Whitehead."

She smiled. "So are we."

Sometimes I hate having a curious mind. But Wendy's smile and the word we instantly burrowed themselves into my brain. I replayed Friday evening again. The Range Rover. Watching Grace sprinting to the bunkhouse. The handwritten maps.

Wendy Whitehead could see my gears grinding. "It looks like you've almost figured it out, Mr. McSwain. Just remember, my husband didn't like partying all alone in his ivory tower."

Wendy looked at Grace, who seemed anxious. "Don't worry, sweetheart. He won't tell. He's on our side." She turned her attention back to me. "Isn't that right, Mr. McSwain?"

I froze as the whole scenario played in my head. Wendy, Grace, and Jake plotting the insurance scam in the bunkhouse, right above the bounty. Jake emptying the safe and burying its contents. Jake speeding back to the bunkhouse in the UTV after getting a radio call from Grace saying there was an emergency. She and Wendy telling him it was prison or the gun.

Grace wouldn't see any of the insurance money, but Wendy was about to get half of George's cash and assets. That'd be more than enough to keep the ranch going.

Jake's punishment seemed harsh to me. But if these two women—both of whom worked hard to make this world a little better—deemed it appropriate, who was I to judge? Perhaps the cheating was only part of the reason. Either way, the way they stuck it to Jake and George made me hopeful that justice really can get served to those above the law.

There was still one loose thread, though. Well, two, actually. But as I opened my mouth to ask, Wendy tapped her collarbone—right beside a diamond necklace. I looked over at Grace, who was wearing its twin.

Grace winked at me, then turned to greet the next person in line.

THE FINAL COUNTDOWN

I asked for this. For the prairie grass scratching at my upper ankles, evading the sneakers and socks. For the sound of snakes and other creatures rustling through that grass as I slog toward an abandoned farmhouse.

For the task of making sure a squatter doesn't live here. Or, worse, an isolationist who'd rather spend money on drugs and drink than home repairs and landscaping.

I met him a week ago, a manic skeleton who threatened to sic his dog on me. The large black Chow looked friendly enough until hearing from its master. In the end, he provided the one answer I truly needed before I backed off his property.

These are the kinds of challenging cases I requested. And why wouldn't I? More hours. More mileage. More money. As a thirtysomething woman who's been fired and divorced over the last year, I need every nickel I can mine out of the Texas hardpan.

So I creep closer to the house, a graying wooden home still surrounded by evergreens to break the Panhandle wind.

I intend to knock on the door and ensure nobody's home to interview, but the sound comes before I reach the door—a million insects at work. And not the crickets I'm used to hearing near dusk—especially out in fields northeast of Amarillo and southwest of nowhere—but a horde of flies, orbiting the poor antelope that couldn't find its way out.

I might've left then, marked the house abandoned and called it a night. But as I turn, my brain finally isolates the stench, now unmistakable as it is foul.

I DID NOT ask for this. Not the talking to the sheriff's deputy. Not the late-summer insects feasting on my shins as the sun falls victim to a flat horizon.

And certainly not the body rolling past me under a white sheet.

Though macabre, I wonder whether I'm still on the clock. I pull out my work cell—a government-issued iPhone with a Dallas area code and internet restrictions—and text my supervisor.

Still here. Waiting for investigator. How do I handle my timesheet?

If standing near a possible crime scene didn't count as work, I'd miss out on an hour's overtime. Only thirty-five bucks, but I need every dime of it.

Three dots are still dancing on the screen when Matthew McConoughey yips a not-at-all fluent hola because he thinks I'm Hispanic. Though that's what I want him—and everyone else—to think. It's what I believed until a DNA test told me I was part Comanche. And that revelation landed me here, waiting to talk to a man about a dead body rather than hunting down the killer.

Mr. Hola is older and much heavier than the actor, gingerly crossing a nearby cattle guard.

"So, you're the lucky lady who found the DB," he says, not bothering to translate the cop jargon despite the fact I'm a civilian. It's a new-ish title.

I nod. "Yessir. I'm working for ..."

"I've been briefed, Mrs. Reynolds."

I'm not sure what my face does upon hearing that name, but it must adequately convey my mixture of confusion and disgust.

"Oh, that's right. My condolences on the divorce. Got one of those myself, though that was a long time ago now."

This man, who I can only assume is a Texas Ranger, is talking as though we were old friends. Before I respond, my brain has done its thing, and I place his voice.

I don't have a photographic memory. It's more like a voice recorder in my head that I can't shut off or delete. Ever. And even my voice gets stored forever. Nobody knows this but me, and I work hard to keep it that way—especially now that I'd rather be left alone than engage in conversation about my malfunctioning mind.

He continues his slow but steady march toward me before stopping about ten yards away. "I don't think we ever met in person, just on a conference call. I'm Lieutenant William Cody. But most people call me—"

"Buffalo Bill."

I maintain control over my facial muscles, but he doesn't need a visible reaction to smile at my embarrassment. The last time I worked with the Rangers, I called Lt. Cody something I hope never to repeat.

I was off the force a few months later. My outburst wasn't the reason, though it surely didn't help.

"So it's back to Lori Young, then?"

I nod.

"Well, Ms. Young, I have to wonder about the odds of a former Amarillo homicide detective catching a case nearly two hours from home." He motions to the cornfields surrounding us. "And in the middle of nowhere."

"Probably the same odds as a man named William Cody owning a ranch with a herd of bison."

This time his smile is friendly. "You'll understand if we get your prints and a swab to rule you out."

I motion to the CSI van, now occupied by the body. "They have everything in there? Or will I have to drive to Dumas?"

"We can take care of it here. Shouldn't take long." He steps closer, and I am careful not to edge backward. "While we wait, can I get some proof that you were here on official business?"

I pull out the work cell—a green banner informs me that no, I am not getting paid to talk with Buffalo Bill—and open the government app. After navigating to a GPS map, I close the distance between us and zoom in on our location.

"The blue dot is us," I say, "and the blue pin is the house." I tap on the icon, and it pulls up the address, though it only gives the farm-to-market road and a descriptor: OLD WOOD HSE LRG WNDWS.

"All right then, I'll round up the techs so we can get you home at a decent hour." He whistles using his thumb and index finger, then waves one of the men in white jumpsuits our way.

I HAVE ONE final ask. As we begin the trek toward our respective pickups, I insert myself into the case despite having been stripped of any right to professional courtesy.

"Any idea who he was?"

He's silent for a few steps while considering my inquiry. A nod finally lets me know whatever he's heard about my abrupt dismissal from the APD isn't enough to keep him from humoring me.

"Won't get a positive ID for a bit, but all indications are he's the man wanted for robbing that Allsup's in Stinnett."

I take a moment to recall the case. Though I recall all the TV news coverage verbatim, I frame my next statement like a question. It helps keep people from asking about my ... condition. "He and the clerk opened fire on each other, right?"

"Right," he says, motioning me to continue toward our vehicles on the other side of the cattle guard. "Third time this year after the state started encouraging armed cashiers. Anyway, our guy was hit but still managed to haul hind tail north on 136. Locals found the old Firebird he was driving abandoned in a cornfield. There was plenty of blood inside, but their canines lost the scent a mile or so out."

I laugh as we approach our respective pickups during twilight's last gasp. "Wonder if I still get to collect the store's reward money. I don't remember the wanted poster saying dead or alive." I'm not lying this time. I never bothered to read the specifics aloud. In fact, I was more than happy to let active law enforcement officers handle a case for once.

Buffalo Bill shakes his head. "You'll have to take that up with them. I do know you've made my life a little harder."

"How's that?"

"I'm going to catch a lot of grief for letting a fugitive hide a mile from where I sleep every night." He points to a two-story house just down the road. "I'm surprised my own dogs didn't flush him out."

I've read the list of houses aloud to myself and know Buffalo Bill was next. "Looks like I was going to come see you this evening either way," I say while palming the phone. "You want to get this out of the way?"

He checks his watch. "Can you do it in less than five minutes?"

I'm already tapping the screen as I answer in the affirmative. "What's your middle name, Mr. William Cody?"

"Robert."

"And how many people live at your house?"

"Just me and my wife."

He provides her name and their birthdates. Then I prepare for the less routine questions.

"These next questions are about race and ethnicity. Are either of you of Hispanic origin?"

"I'm not, but my wife is. She's Mexican American."

I continue nodding and tapping. "Now, for the 2025 Texas Census, Hispanic is an ethnicity and not a race, so you're both considered Caucasian."

He nods, checks his watch again.

"Just two more questions," I say, returning the phone to my back pocket, knowing I can remember his answer and record it after I get in my truck. "Do you both plan on remaining in The Republic for at least the next two years?"

"Absolutely. No better place on God's green earth."

I mumble in agreement. "And would you like to sponsor a family member's move from any other country?"

"No. We thought about having my mother-in-law come down from Durango, but she says she's fine."

"I bet," I say. "The Free State of Southwestern Colorado is basically the Wild Wild West. No rules. No taxes."

"No place for a woman in her eighties, you ask me. But I'm letting my wife handle that. It'll be a lot of immigration paperwork, but we can always bring her down later."

I nod and thank Buffalo Bill for his time, then close out his case in the cab of my dually.

Before starting my journey home, I let the darkness settle over me. I wonder if folks are doing this in every other country across North America, helping count its current and prospective residents.

Preparing for the Future. That's the slogan for us Texas enumerators, printed right there on the back of our phone cases.

But I'm not fooled. I'm not readying for a new beginning.

I'm counting down to the end.

NOTE: This short story is a prequel of sorts to my novel DIVIDED STATES, *which can be ordered wherever you buy your books.*

NOTE FROM THE AUTHOR

All of these short stories were previously published in anthologies compiled and edited by my local writing club, the Texas High Plains Writers. Founded as Panhandle Pen Women in 1920, this organization is the oldest of its kind in Texas and one of the oldest in the nation. I encourage you all to learn more about THPW and to peruse all of their anthologies, which can be found on Amazon.

ABOUT THE AUTHOR

Rick Treon writes about life and death in the Lone Star State.

His 2022 novel, the speculative action thriller *Divided States,* won the PenCraft Award for Literary Excellence in Thrillers and was shortlisted for the Silver Falchion Award and Best Thriller Book Award.

Rick's debut, *Deep Background*, won the 2019 PenCraft Award for Literary Excellence in

Suspense, and his second novel, *Let the Guilty Pay,* was nominated for the 2021 Silver Falchion Award for Best Suspense Novel and the PenCraft Award for Literary Excellence in Suspense.

Rick was named Writer of the Year in 2021 by the Texas High Plains Writers.

Before making up stories, he worked as a reporter and top editor for several newspapers in Texas, where he still lives and writes.

Visit ricktreon.com for more.